For Steve.
"Shyness is nice,
but shyness can stop you."
– bb

Little Boost is published by
Picture Window Books
A Capstone Imprint
151 Good Counsel Drive, P.O. Box 669
Mankato, Minnesota 56002
www.capstonepub.com

Library of Congress Cataloging-in-Publication Data
Bracken, Beth.
  Too shy for show-and-tell / by Beth Bracken ; illustrated by
Jennifer Bell.
    p. cm. – (Little boost)
Summary: Sam is so shy that nobody knows much about him,
but when he must stand in front of his class for show-and-tell,
he finds the courage to share.
  ISBN 978-1-4048-6654-6 (library binding)
[1. Bashfulness–Fiction. 2. Show-and-tell presentations–Fiction.
3. Schools–Fiction.] I. Bell, Jennifer A., ill. II. Title. III. Series.
  PZ7.B6989Too 2011
  [E]–dc22   2010050939

Creative Director: Heather Kindseth
Art Director: Kay Fraser
Designer: Emily Harris

Printed in the United States of America in North Mankato, Minnesota.
032011
006110CGF11

Too Shy for Show -and- Tell

by Beth Bracken   illustrated by Jennifer Bell

PICTURE WINDOW BOOKS
a capstone imprint

Sam was a quiet boy.
Nobody knew much about him.

Sam loved trucks, but nobody knew that.

Sam's favorite food was chocolate cake,
but nobody knew that.

Sam thought dogs were the best animals in the world,
but nobody knew that, either.

The only thing that people knew about Sam was that
he didn't talk much.

And Sam really didn't like talking in front of people,
which is why Sam hated show-and-tell.

On the chalkboard: Show-and-Tell Friday

On Wednesday, Miss Emily told the class that show-and-tell would be on Friday.

Sam spent most of Thursday worrying. He had a great thing
to bring for show-and-tell, but he was scared.

On Friday, Sam didn't get out of bed.

"My tummy hurts," he lied.

"You're fine, and you need to go to school today," his mom said.

At school, Sam told Miss Emily he'd forgotten
about show-and-tell.

"I didn't bring anything," he said. But that wasn't true.
His perfect show-and-tell thing was in his backpack.

"That's okay," Miss Emily said. "You can just tell the class
about the thing you forgot at home."

Sam was terrified. He didn't want to talk in front of everyone.
The thought of it made his tummy hurt really, really bad.

He imagined that he'd say something dumb.

Or that he'd mess up his word.

Or that he'd faint.

Or that he'd cry.

Sam watched the other kids show their show-and-tell things.

David showed some socks that his grandma had knitted him.
Everyone clapped when he was done.

Helena showed a new doll she got for her birthday.

Everyone clapped when she was done.

Otto showed a cool leaf that he found on the way to school.

Otto said "weaf" instead of "leaf," but nobody seemed to notice, and everyone clapped when he was done.

Then it was Sam's turn. He got his perfect show-and-tell thing out of his backpack and went to the front of the room.

"What do you have to show us today, Sam?"
Miss Emily asked with a smile.

Sam took a deep breath. He looked out at his classmates. They were quietly waiting.

Sam held up his picture. "This is my new dog," he said.
"I named him Chocolate, because that's my favorite kind
of cake, and he's the color of chocolate cake."

Sam didn't faint.

He didn't throw up.

He didn't cry.

And no one laughed.

Instead, everyone clapped
when he was done.

Now everyone in class knew
a little bit more about Sam.

Next time, he thought,
I'll bring my biggest truck.

And he did.